ready, steady, read!

Puffling in a Pickle

Margaret Ryan
Illustrated by
Trevor Dunton

Puffin Books

PUFFIN BOOKS

Published by the Penguin Group
Penguin Books Ltd, 27 Wrights Lane, London W8 5TZ, England
Penguin Books USA Inc., 375 Hudson Street, New York, New York 10014, USA
Penguin Books Australia Ltd, Ringwood, Victoria, Australia
Penguin Books Canada Ltd, 10 Alcorn Avenue, Toronto, Ontario, Canada M4V 3B2
Penguin Books (NZ) Ltd, 182–190 Wairau Road, Auckland 10, New Zealand

Penguin Books Ltd, Registered Offices: Harmondsworth, Middlesex, England

Published in Puffin Books 1995
10 9 8 7 6

Text copyright © Margaret Ryan, 1995
Illustrations copyright © Trevor Dunton, 1995
All rights reserved

The moral right of the author and illustrator has been asserted

Filmset in Monotype Bembo Schoolbook
Reproduction by Anglia Graphics Ltd, Bedford

Made and printed in Great Britain by Clays Ltd, St Ives plc

Contents

PUFFLING IN A PICKLE

It was Puffling's first day out of the burrow, and he was ready to explore.

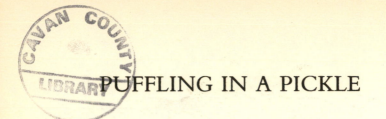

"Don't wander off and get lost,"
said his mum.

"I won't," said Puffling.

"Remember to stay close to
home," said his dad.

"I will," said Puffling.

And he really meant to.

But he forgot.

There were so many interesting
things to see elsewhere. First,
there was a very interesting cliff
top to peer over.

"What a long way down to the
beach," said Puffling, waving to
the seals below.

Then there was a very interesting empty crisp packet to investigate; till it blew away in the wind.

"Come back," squawked Puffling, and chased after it.

Finally, there was a big grassy hill
to climb.

"I wonder what's on the
other side," said Puffling,
and puffed up the hill to
see.

All he saw was the other side of
the grassy hill.

"Well, that's not very
interesting," said Puffling. "I
think I'll go home
now."

He waddled back down the hill
and looked at all the burrows.

"Now which one is mine?" he
wondered. "There are so many . . .

I think it might be this one."

He poked his fluffy head down
to see.

"Mum," he called, "are you in
there?"

"I'm not your mum, you silly bird," squawked a very cross puffin. "Go and find your own burrow, and stop poking your beak down other people's. What a cheek. Really, young birds these days . . . no manners at all."

"Sorry," said Puffling, and scuttled away.

He wandered on till he found
another burrow that looked
familiar.

"Maybe this is mine," he said.

He poked his fluffy head down
to see.

"Mum, Dad, are you in there?" he called.

"What a silly billy bird," scoffed a family of rabbits. "Are you blind? Do we look like your mum and dad? Do we have wings? Do we have feathers? Do we have orange beaks?"

"No, but you do rabbit on a bit,"
muttered Puffling, and scuttled
away.

Puffling wandered on till he came
to quite a large burrow near the
cliff.

"I don't know if this is my burrow or not," he panted, "but I think I'll just slip inside for a rest anyway. I'm tired out with all this exploring."

He went down into the burrow
and called, "Mum? Dad? Is there
anybody in there?"

"Who wants to know?"
answered an oily voice.

"Me, Puffling. I'm tired out. I'm looking for my burrow, and I can't find it anywhere. I think it's lost."

"Oh, what a shame," said the oily voice. "Come on in, and rest yourself, little Puffling. You'll be very comfortable in here, and you're VERY welcome."

"Thank you," said Puffling, and
went on in.

Then he saw whose
burrow it was.

"Sly fox!" he yelled, and turned
and ran outside.

Sly fox bounded after him.

"Come back, little Puffling," he
called. "You'll be just right for my
dinner."

"Oh no, he won't," squawked a familiar voice, and Puffling's dad dropped down from the sky, and nipped sly fox on the nose.

"OOOOOOWWWWLLLL!"

"This way, Puffling," squawked his mum. "FLY!"

And Puffling flew, his little wings flapping as fast as they would go.

"Whew, that was a lucky escape,"
said his dad when they were all
safely back inside their own
burrow.

"I thought I told you not to wander off and get lost, Puffling," said his mum. "Your dad and I have been out looking for you for ages."

"I'm sorry," said Puffling. "I tried to get home, but then all the burrows looked the same."

"I have an idea," said his dad.
"Come outside . . .

See that big tree over there . . . ?"
Puffling nodded.

"Well, our burrow is the third one
on the left after the big tree.
Right?"

"No, left," grinned Puffling.

PUFFLING GOES FISHING

Puffling poked his fluffy head out
of his burrow.

"I'm feeling a bit peckish," he
said to his mum. "Can I go down
to the seashore and see if Little
Seal wants to go fishing?"

"All right," said his mum. "But don't get lost like you did the other day. Remember we live in the third burrow on the left, after the big tree."

"I'll remember," said Puffling.

Puffling took a flying leap into the
air at the edge of the rocky cliff,
and flapped down on to the beach
below.

He skidded to a sandy halt beside
Little Seal, who was snuggled up
close to her mum.

Little Seal had her eyes closed.

"You asleep, Little Seal?" asked
Puffling, poking her with his beak.

"Not now, I'm not," muttered
Little Seal.

"I'm feeling a bit peckish," said
Puffling. "Want to go fishing?"
    Little Seal wriggled and
yawned. "Come to think of it, I'm
feeling a bit peckish too. Can I go
fishing with Puffling, Mum?"

"All right," said her mum. "But don't get lost like Puffling did the other day. Remember where I'm lying; right here, beside the grey rock with the barnacles on it."

"We'll remember," said Little Seal and Puffling together.

Puffling and Little Seal hurried
down to the water's edge.

"Bet I'm first to catch a fish,"
squawked Puffling.

"Bet you're not," snorted Little
Seal. "You're still hopeless at
fishing."

In the first three minutes, Little
Seal caught three fish. In the first
three minutes Puffling caught . . .

a big crab which nipped his leg . . .

a jellyfish which tasted awful . . .

and a piece of clingy seaweed,
which wrapped itself round and
round him till he was all tied up
like a parcel . . .

Little Seal had to help untangle
him, then they both bobbed back
up to the surface.

"Whew, thanks, Little Seal," puffed Puffling. "That was a lucky escape. I still haven't caught any fish yet, and now I'm not just peckish, I'm absolutely starving!"

"Look," said Little Seal, "here comes another shoal of fish. Even you should be able to catch some of them. Follow me, and do what I do."

Puffling followed Little Seal, did what she did, and was amazed when he caught a mouthful of fish.

The pair of them bobbed back
up to the surface again, and
Puffling was so excited at his
catch, he opened his mouth and
squawked . . .

"Look at all the fish I've caught,
Little Seal . . ."

"Not now, you haven't," laughed
Little Seal, as all the fish wriggled
from Puffling's open beak and
swam away.

"Oh no," wailed Puffling. "After
all that hard work too, and I'm
still starving. I'm fed up with this
rotten fishing. I'm going home."

He trailed back up the beach to
the grey rock with the barnacles
on it, said goodbye to Little Seal,
then flapped back up the cliff face
to the first, no, the second, no, the
third burrow on the left after the
big tree.

"Oh good, you're back, Puffling,"
said his mum. "You didn't get lost
today."

"*I* didn't get lost," huffed
Puffling, "but I lost my fish. I just
opened my beak to speak to Little
Seal, and all the fish I'd caught
wriggled out, and swam away."

"Never mind," said his mum. "I
went fishing too. I've brought you
something to eat."

"I hope it's not a crab, or a
jellyfish, or some clingy seaweed,"
moaned Puffling.

"Of course not," laughed his mum. "It's fish."

"Yummy," said Puffling.

"I thought you'd like that," said his mum, and passed him a whole beakful.

Puffling nodded his fluffy head in reply, but said nothing. This time he was holding on to his fish. This time he was keeping his beak tightly shut.

ready, steady, read!